CinderAlf

by

Lynne Markham

Illustrated by Alan Marks

You do not need to read this page -
just get on with the book!

First published 2002 in Great Britain by
Barrington Stoke Ltd
10 Belford Terrace, Edinburgh, EH4 3DQ

Printed by Polestar AUP Aberdeen Ltd

MEET THE AUTHOR - LYNNE MARKHAM

What is your favourite animal?
Cat
What is your favourite boy's name?
James
What is your favourite girl's name?
Helena
What is your favourite food?
Bacon
What is your favourite music?
Bach
What is your favourite hobby?
Gardening

MEET THE ILLUSTRATOR - ALAN MARKS

What is your favourite animal?
A snow leopard
What is your favourite boy's name?
Thomas
What is your favourite girl's name?
Kate
What is your favourite food?
Oysters
What is your favourite music?
Mozart
What is your favourite hobby?
Cooking

Contents

Chapter 1
The Wooden Leg

My grandad looks ordinary until he goes to bed at night. Then he unscrews his wooden leg and props it against the end of the bed. The foot still has a brown sock on it and a brown lace-up shoe. When I ask him what happened to his *real* leg he just shakes his head.

"Did he lose it in the war?" I ask Mum. I imagine him being shot down by an enemy, crawling to safety on his belly. Maybe rescuing a mate at the same time.

"No, he was too young to be in the war," says Mum. Her face goes pink. "It was an accident."

"What sort of accident?" I thought his leg might have been bitten off by a crocodile when he was in Africa. Or he'd lost it crashing a motorbike. Or falling out of an aeroplane.

"Never you mind," says Mum.

My younger brother Joe says the leg gives him the creeps. He says it comes alive at night when we're all in bed and goes marching round the house.

"Ker-thump! Ker-thump! Grandad's leg is on the move. The aliens sent it! It's a secret weapon. If you touch it when it's on the march you'll go up in flames!"

I don't believe anything my brother Joe says because he's stupid. He's a thief as well. He nicks my BMX to play with his mates. He breaks the wings off my Buzz Lightyear. He steals the flag from my space station. But worst of all, he nicks my friends.

When he nicked Pete, that's when I flipped. Pete was my best mate until he met Joe. We were always together, kicking a ball or riding our bikes. We pricked our fingers with a rusty pin. That made us blood brothers. We swore to be friends until the day we died. Pete was the brother I *wanted* to have. Until we bumped into Joe in the park one day.

He was surfing a skateboard, which he'd nicked from me of course, and was doing all the jumps and turns. He gave Pete a go on it and then another. He was laughing all the time and fooling around. Doing a double twist on one leg.

Pete was hooked. He didn't care that it was my skateboard. He kept laughing with Joe and punching his shoulder. Telling Joe what a great guy he was. They forgot about me until it was time to go home.

"You coming?" Pete said when it was nearly dark. Then he turned away and ran after Joe. I watched him vanish through the big park gates. After that Pete was out with Joe all the time.

"You can come with us if you *want* to," Joe said, grinning.

Like I needed to be *invited* to go with *my* mate!

I was so furious I wanted to murder Joe. I wanted to dunk his head in boiling oil. I wanted to smash my fist in his stupid face. I wanted to make sure nobody liked him again.

Instead of that I went storming upstairs. I crashed into the first room I came to and found I was crying.

"I hate him!" I yelled. I kicked at the door. "Everyone likes him better than me! It's not fair! He can do what he likes and people think he's cool! Well, this time I'm *really* going to get him!"

I expect I'd been yelling for quite a while, and snuffling and bashing the wall with my fist. Suddenly this quiet voice says, "Don't do that, Mick. You'll hurt yourself."

I whipped round. I was in Grandad's room. He was sitting in an armchair by the window. He had a look on his face I'd not seen before.

"Never say you hate your brother," he said. "Think what it would be like if you were on your own."

"It'd be great!" I said. "I'd be Number One! I'd get to keep all my own stuff! There'd be loads of people who liked me best! There wouldn't be a Joe to nick my friends!"

"Sit down, son." Grandad patted the bed next to his chair.

I sat down with a thump and wiped my nose on my hand. I stopped crying but I was still mad. I wanted to zap Joe off the face of the earth. I never wanted to see him again.

Grandad leaned forward to stare into my face. The sun behind him made his eyes look dark. For a moment I was almost scared.

When Grandad spoke again there was a sigh in his voice. He said softly, "You said there wouldn't be a Joe. Well. Imagine there wasn't. Imagine there was no-one on your side. No-one you could count on when the chips were down and you were in for it. Imagine you were *really* on your own."

"Yeah!" I muttered. "It'd be great!"

Only it didn't feel that great now. Maybe it was Grandad's serious voice that made the anger die right down. Or maybe it was because the sun had moved off the room, that I suddenly found myself shivering with cold.

"It might not be so great to be alone," Grandad said. "It might be hell. I know, you see. I was an only child, with no brother or sister. My parents died in a car crash when I was eight, three or four years younger than you are now. I was an orphan. That was just before the war started. I had no-one to call my own. Until one day something happened that changed everything. It was an odd kind of love at first sight."

Grandad sat back in his chair, which gave a creak. He passed a hand across his face.

When he spoke again it was like he wasn't talking to me. As if he'd gone off somewhere – to a place I couldn't reach.

"Listen to me," he said. "I want to tell you something. I want to tell you how I came to lose my leg."

Chapter 2
CinderAlf

I stared at Grandad. I felt scared, I don't know why. But I was excited as well.

"What happened?" I asked. My voice came out like a squeak.

Grandad looked out of the window. He sighed again, as if he were sighing out his memories.

"Well. I told you that I was an orphan. I was sent to live with my Aunty Vera and Uncle Stan who lived in a mining town near Nottingham. They didn't want me, especially Aunty Vera. They had two children already, you see. Two big boys called Eric and Brian.

"Uncle Stan wasn't all that bad. Mostly he just kept out of the way. But Aunty Vera hated me. She said I cost money. Money that should be spent on their two lads. She didn't even want me to wear their cast-off clothes. She said she could sell them for good money. She didn't even want me to breathe the same air as Eric and Brian. Every mouthful of food I ate was a stone in her heart, as if I had stolen it from her boys.

"Then one day she caught me scraping up some food that Eric had left on his plate. It was cold meat pie and cold gravy.

'What do you think *you're* doing?' she roared. She had a voice like coal rolling down into the cellar and a black and evil soul to match. 'Thieves must be punished! Fetch me my pen!'

"Aunty wrote I AM A THIEF in big, black letters and hung it round my neck. I had to wear that sign all day.

"Eric and Brian felt sorry for me. They weren't bad lads. Most of the time they didn't notice me. They were twins and didn't need anyone else.

'Why don't you take it off?' they asked.

"Aunty Vera never got mad with them. They'd never seen into her black heart. They thought I was a coward for keeping it on. But I was scared stiff of Aunty. She used to say things when we were on our own.

'You're a parasite,' she'd hiss. 'You should be put away. You're a useless blood-sucker. Get out of my sight.'

"I thought a parasite was some kind of snake. I imagined I was sprouting slimy, green scales. When she turned away I used to check my legs, just to make sure they were still there.

"I tried to keep away from her. But it was almost as if she could sniff me out. She always found me. She'd come up behind me and grab my collar. Her arms were like great twists of metal. Her fingernails dug into my neck like knives.

'It's time to skin a rabbit,' she'd say.

"That was the thing I hated most. It happened on Wednesdays. Aunty would buy a rabbit from the butcher's shop. The rabbit would be grey and sad-looking. Its poor, dead eyes would still be open. Its paws would hang limp, the soft fur looked dull.

"My job was to help her skin it. As I tore the skin from the flesh, it sounded like a scream. I reckon it was the same scream I wanted to make. But it was coming from that dead rabbit.

'Ooh, wizard!' said Eric and Brian when they saw what we had been doing. They loved rabbit stew. They never saw the revolting bits. But I couldn't touch the stew. I'd go to bed hungry for the next two nights.

"My other job was to clean the grate and sweep out the ashes when we'd had a fire. That was all right. I'd get my arms and face all covered with ash, but I didn't care. Brian said I looked like a grey-haired old man, but Eric said, 'Nah! He doesn't. He looks for all the world like CinderAlf.'

"My name was Alfred, d'you see? And I did all the Cinderella chores. They didn't mean to be unkind. They didn't mean anything. They just never thought. Except about each other, that is. And somehow that name stuck to me. I was CinderAlf from that day on.

"Well," Grandad looked out of the window at a bird flying past. When he turned back again his face was bleak. "I was lonely, right? I'd got no-one. Or else I might not have done what I did that day.

"It was a Tuesday morning if I remember right. I was up real early to clear out the grate. The ash had turned my hair pale grey. There was a pale, grey light coming in from outside. Everyone else was still in bed. I could hear Uncle Stan snoring and Aunty coughing. The twins' beds creaked over my head.

"Suddenly this ray of sun streaked in. I looked out at the yard. You could see a green tree poking up over the wall. There was a patch of blue sky. The day looked too beautiful to stay indoors. All I wanted was to get outside.

"I finished my chores and listened hard. I could still hear the coughing and snoring and creaking from upstairs, so I reckoned I was safe to go out for a while.

"I crept to the back door and drew back the bolt. It made a noise like a gun going off. I thought Aunty Vera might appear in her curlers and her enormous, flapping nightgown.

"But none of them woke up, and in another minute I was in the back yard.

"I nipped over the wall. My heart was pumping like a steam engine. I could hear the chuffing sound it made in my head. If Aunty caught me she'd kill me and skin me like that dead rabbit. She'd serve my head up on a big white plate. But what I heard next was a song thrush calling from a tall tree. It seemed like a sign that something good was going to happen.

"I went down the street, but I was going nowhere. I was walking for the sake of it. Just because it was sunny and spring. No-one else was about that early. The milkman hadn't begun to deliver. The night-shift hadn't come up from the pit yet.

"I started to sing. Then I ran for a bit. I turned cart-wheels. I frisked like a horse let out in a meadow. When I stopped I was gasping but I felt real good. The chuffing noise had gone from my head. I couldn't hear the thrush any more, but I could hear something else.

"At first I thought it was someone laughing, *chuck-chuck-chuckle*. Or a hen chuntering in a back yard. The sound seemed to be coming from a shop nearby.

"I went up to the window and looked inside. There was a pile of bright red cocoa tins on display, and some bars of soap that were a pale pea-green.

"The shop was still closed but the sound got louder– *chuck-chuck-CHUCKLE-CHUCK!* I went round the side to the big glass door. In front of it there was a carrier bag. It was made out of paper that you couldn't see through.

"The bag had string for handles and writing down the side: *Marsden's Cakes – the finest in town.*

"There was a drawing on it of a cake with a single candle.

"I went up to the carrier bag and the chuckling noise stopped. It went dead quiet.

The thought came to me that something amazing was about to happen.

"When I leaned forward, I was shaking all over. But at first I couldn't make anything out. There was just a white blob moving. Then the blob became two legs and two arms. I saw a head covered with a pink woolly hat, and two round blue eyes. After that the chuckling sound started again.

"Shush," I said, under my breath. "Shush. It's all right. I'm here now.

"I was still shaking when I picked up the baby from the bag and held her for the first time in my arms."

Chapter 3
CinderElla

"A baby!" I said to Grandad, who had paused in his story. I was disgusted. I'd expected something more exciting than that. Babies are nasty, smelly, squirmy things.

Grandad went on with his story, just as if I hadn't spoken. "She was beautiful. I could see that, even though her face was red and she'd a tiny fist stuck in her mouth. When I picked her up she stopped chuckling again. She stared at me out of her big, blue eyes. That's when I knew we were meant to be together. There was even a note saying so attached to her jumper. It said: *Please take care of my little girl. I can't.*

"When I read the note I got this lump in my chest, a kind of terrible sadness. Nobody wanted the baby. She had been thrown away like a bag of rubbish. She hadn't a friend in the world. She was on her own – like me.

"The lump in my chest got bigger and bigger. Then it burst and I got this smashing idea. I decided I would keep the baby. I knew she wasn't my own flesh and blood. She was better than that. Better than Aunty Vera and

Uncle Stan and the twins. She somehow made the world seem grand.

"I put her back in the carrier bag. I noticed there was a baby's bottle in there. I picked up the bag and clutched it to my chest.

"After that, I set off down the street. At first, I didn't know where I was going. I just walked and walked. I could feel the baby bumping about in the bag, but she didn't start to cry. She seemed to know what I was doing and that I was going to take care of her.

"By then the street was beginning to wake up. The milkman was clinking bottles about. Miners were stomping home from the pits. You could hear the tram rattle down the line. It made me afraid I might be seen. That Aunty Vera would suddenly appear with her nightie flapping like a witch's cloak. She'd haul me off by the scruff of the neck and I'd never see the baby again.

"I walked faster and faster. Sweat was trickling down my ribs and my long, woolly socks were falling down. I still didn't know where I was going, but when I turned a corner I saw some garden allotments. You could see empty bean rows poking up at the sky and sheds made out of scraps of wood and old front doors.

"I slowed down. Some of the allotments had been abandoned. One of them had a shed on it.

"I walked up to it and went inside. An empty crate on the floor said BEST BANANAS. I lowered the baby into it. It was just the right size for her. When she was in it she kicked her legs up and laughed.

"I was that chuffed I started to grin myself! I had always wanted the world to be wonderful and now it was. There was someone who needed me. Someone special who had been sent!

"When she fell asleep, I tip-toed out of the shed and went home. I jumped up and down on the way. I wanted to break out into a song but I didn't dare, just in case I was heard. When I got home Aunty Vera was there.

'What have *you* been up to?' she asked, peering. She couldn't bear for me to be happy, not ever. She thought I was stealing it from her.

"After that I calmed myself down. I ate a slice of bread and dripping and put the other slice in my pocket. Then I washed the dishes and set off for school.

"Only I never got there. Instead I went back to the shed. And the baby was still fast asleep in her crate. I kept looking at her. I was amazed that she could really be mine.

"But what she needed now was a proper name. I thought of Susan and Sarah and Jane. None of them sounded exactly right. Then I remembered that she was unwanted like me.

"It made me decide I would call her Ella. We'd be Cinder*Alf* and Cinder*Ella*. It was like being a real blood brother and sister. We'd belong together for evermore.

"I touched her face very gently with my finger. Then I said her name out loud for the first time. 'Ella.' It made me frightened for us all at once. I didn't know very much about babies.

"How would I look after her? How would I get her food and clothes? How would I make sure she stayed properly hidden?

"And what would happen if Aunty Vera found out?"

Chapter 4
In the Woods

"Did Aunty Vera find out?" I asked.

"She might have done," Grandad said. "But before she could we ran off to the woods. It was before they built that new estate. There were woods all around us then."

"Wicked!" I said.

I pictured the woods like Sherwood Forest. They would be dark and deep. You could have a gang and shoot bows and arrows. You could make a fire out of twigs and leaves. Everything would be one big laugh.

"It wasn't like that," Grandad replied, as if I'd spoken out loud. "It wasn't like a great adventure. It was hard. We were hungry all the time.

"I made a small shelter for us out of branches and bracken that were lying around. I had got chilblains from the cold and my fingers were all red and cracked. My hands bled all the time we were in the woods.

"After that, I made Ella a cradle, just soft earth hollowed out and lined with moss. She looked a treat in it.

"But I was scared to leave her there in case someone found her. Sometimes people walked their dogs in the woods. There was talk of the army camping there. But what could I do? There was nowhere else.

"I left her every day while I went out and stole. I stole a blanket and some nappies off a line. I stole loaves of bread from the baker's van. I stole milk from doorsteps and fruit off allotments. I stole eggs from a hen house in a farmer's field.

"No-one seemed to be looking for me. I reckoned Aunty Vera would be glad to be rid of me. The woods were empty. All you could hear were animals rustling, and trees shushing in the breeze.

"It rained a lot. I had to steal an umbrella for us. That was the time I nearly got caught.

"I saw some umbrellas near an open door and I crept to the stand and took hold of one. When I did, I heard this yell.

'You, boy! What are you doing there? Parker! Come quickly – we have a thief!'

"The voice belonged to a lady. But a great big man in a dark suit came out of a room. He had thick, black hair and a black, hairy face.

"You little devil!" he yelled at me in a posh voice. "I'll beat you black and blue when I catch you!"

"He lunged forward at me but I was quicker than him. I shot out of the door but I kept the umbrella. After that I ran like the wind. In and out of alleyways. Over the slippery, rough cobblestones of the back streets.

"When I slowed down I was somewhere I didn't know. My heart was beating *badum-badum.* I was laughing, but I didn't know what I was laughing at. Ha-ha-ha! Hee-hee-hee! People in the street were looking at me but I couldn't stop.

"In the end, I saw a policeman coming towards me. I don't reckon he was coming for me, but I thought he was. So I ran again and this time I finished up back at the woods.

"For the rest of the day, I was too scared to go out. We sat under the umbrella, me and Ella, and listened to the trees drip.

"That night we were both too hungry to sleep. She was crying all the time.

"A few days later something else happened. I'd gone out to look for food again, but most of the milk had been taken in. It had stopped raining and was getting warmer.

People didn't want their milk to go off in the sun.

"It meant I had to go further than usual to look for some. I walked and walked.

"In the end I came to a cluster of shops. One of them was a Post Office. There was a big, red letterbox outside on the pavement. On the wall there was a board with a poster pinned up.

"I glanced at the board as I went past, and then swerved back and stood stock-still. My feet felt like they were nailed to the ground. My chest felt like it had just been punched.

"The poster said, WANTED – HAVE YOU SEEN THIS BOY?

"And underneath, there was a picture of me."

Chapter 5
The Trap

"Wow!" I said. My Grandad was a wanted man! It was nearly as good as getting eaten by a crocodile!

Grandad said, "It was an old photo. The boy looked younger than me, and cleaner. But you could tell it was me. It even had my name underneath: Alfred Packard.

"The photo made me feel sick inside. I felt that everyone was looking at me. Even the old ladies going for stamps. I felt like a criminal.

"I turned round and ran away. I seemed to spend my whole life running. Except when I was with Ella. Then everything slowed down to a soft, sweet pace. Like we were living in another, gentler world.

"After I'd seen the photo, I ran back to Ella. I was coughing while I ran. My chest hurt. When I got back, Ella looked smaller and thinner than ever. Her blanket was damp. Nasty, sore patches flamed on her skin.

"Ella began to cry a lot. Not a loud cry, more a gentle bleating. It was like listening to a hurt animal. The crying broke my heart. When I picked her up, she stopped crying, but you could hear her breathing.

"Her breathing was like mine. The same as old blokes who've been down the pit. It was as if her chest was all furred up. Wheezy and hard. Her nose ran. Her hands felt cold.

"But I still thought we were meant to be together. I couldn't give her up. It would be like cutting off an arm or a leg.

"So I carried on stealing and trying to get her to eat. But she wouldn't. She just coughed and wheezed.

'Come *on*, Ella,' I used to say. 'Eat it, will you? Just for me.'

"I even stole a toy for her. It was a blue velvet dog with long, white ears. The dog lay on her chest like a dead thing.

'What can I *do*?' I asked her, scared.

"I was getting desperate, trying to cuddle her under my shirt. In my heart I knew I had to give her up. But still I might not have done it then. I might not even have done it at all.

"Except something else happened. Something so terrible it's hard to repeat."

Grandad stopped talking all at once. His face went blank and inward-looking. As if he was staring at something I couldn't see.

"What was it?" I whispered. I was nearly too afraid to know.

Grandad spoke again. His voice was fierce and low. "I was out one day and I was stealing eggs.

"I went to a place I'd not been to before. It was a small farm set behind some trees. You could see hens scratching round in a cleared-out space. The hen houses were rotten and falling down.

"I went over the fence and into the trees. The grass under them was nearly waist high. Remember I was small and skinny. I was going carefully, so I wouldn't be seen. I was nearly up to the hens.

"Then suddenly I heard this *crack!* Exactly like a gun going off. After that, there was this pain in my leg. So fierce it nearly made me faint. I looked down and saw I was in a trap.

"The teeth of the trap were clawing at my leg. Blood was running in a thick, bright stream. The pain was – well ..."

Grandad stopped again. He passed a hand across his face.

"... it was like nothing I've felt before or since. I think the teeth had nearly got to the bone.

"I tried to pull the teeth of the trap apart. But they were clenched shut like they were locked in place. I pulled and pulled, but they wouldn't budge. Then I started shouting, 'Help me! Help!'

"No-one came. My voice was that thin and weak. It was more like a lamb bleating than a boy screaming for help.

"I thought I would die right where I was, but then a miracle happened.

"I was pulling feebly at the metal trap when suddenly it gave a click. The teeth came apart an inch or two. It wasn't much. But it was enough for me to wriggle free.

"After that I started to struggle back. My leg was still bleeding and turning blue. I was fighting my way through the grass like it was a jungle and crying and panting as I went.

"Still, I managed to get back to Ella.

"She was quiet when I got there. Not even coughing.

'Ella?' I said. 'Don't fret. I'm here.'

"I took my shirt off and tied it tight around my leg. But it hurt that much it made me catch my breath. And it was coming on to rain again. Without my shirt I was freezing cold.

"I knew we were done for. My leg was swelling. I was coughing my head off. And *my* skin had funny red blotches all over, just like Ella's. I couldn't go out to steal for us.

"I picked Ella up. 'I'm so sorry,' I said.

"I put her back down. I couldn't look at her face. The hurt at leaving her was worse than the pain in my leg.

"It hurts me still when I think about it. It's like a hole inside me that never got mended.

"I crawled away. Somehow I managed to get to some shops. When I crawled in the doorway everyone looked.

"The shopkeeper paused with his hands on the till. A lady pulled her skirt away from me.

'I'm the boy on the poster,' I said.

"The lady gave a piercing scream.

"After that, I reckon all hell broke loose."

Chapter 6
In Hospital

Grandad stopped again. He seemed to be drowning in a great black pool of sadness. "Well," he said at last. "They called the police and an ambulance. The police car came with its bell ringing.

"The shopkeeper made a fuss of me. 'You've been in the newspapers for the last two weeks. Everyone thought you were dead,' he said.

"The ambulance came. They put a blanket round me. But I wouldn't let them take me away.

'You've got to go and find Ella!' I said.

"They thought the pain had gone to my head. That I was rambling in my mind and didn't know what I was saying.

'Shush,' they said. 'It'll be all right.'

"They picked me up but I kicked and bit. 'Find Ella!' I said. 'She's in the woods. Let me go and I'll take you there.'

"Well, of course they didn't know about Ella. They thought I was just making her up.

"But I kicked and yelled until I was blue in the face. In the end they decided to go along with me. They put me in a black police car with an ambulance following on behind.

'Right. Take us to this kid,' they said. And they smiled to each other over my head.

"We drove and drove down all the wrong roads. I was confused and angry. I was in pain. I couldn't find the right way. Everything looked different from a police car.

"When we got to the woods I hobbled out. A policeman had to hold me up. We pushed our way through trees and shrubs until we came to where Ella was.

"I heard her bleating, but I still didn't look.

'Poor, little thing!' a policeman gasped.

"The words were like a knife in my heart.

"I was too sad even to cry for her.

"They wrapped her up and took her away to the waiting ambulance. I didn't go with her, I just stood there, shocked and stunned.

'Come on, lad,' they said. 'Your turn now.' But I wouldn't move until Ella had gone.

"I knew, you see, that we were finished for good. That when she got to the hospital she'd be taken away from me. That I wouldn't see her, ever again.

"And it was hard, our lad, I'm telling you that.

"Later, I let them take me off. I went to the hospital, to a big children's ward with pictures of fairytales on the walls. I lay in bed with my leg throbbing, but they said they'd got to cure my chest.

"How's Ella?" I kept asking, over and over again.

'She's doing well. She's gaining weight. You just try to get yourself well.'

"When my chest was better they said my leg had to go.

'It's so badly infected that gangrene's set in. I'm sorry, son.'

"They cut it off. I didn't care. Without Ella nothing mattered much.

"Aunty Vera came to see me with Eric and Brian. The three of them seemed to fill the ward. Aunty stared at me with her mean little eyes. Then she thrust her face in front of mine.

"She said, 'Don't think I'll have you back to live with us! You're a bad lot. You'll come to a sticky end. I'm not going to feed and clothe you any more. So make your mind up to that, my lad.'

"Brian and Eric just shuffled their feet and looked embarrassed at their mum.

'Sorry, mate,' Eric said when they left. I never saw either of them again.

"Well. I didn't *want* to go back and live with them. But what were they going to do with me?

"I still didn't care. I was weak and depressed. I kept seeing Ella in my imagination. In my dreams I would hear her cry.

"One day they told me she'd been adopted.

'A really nice couple,' was what they said. 'Don't fret. She'll have a really good life.'

"It was the best I could hope for, but I was still miserable. I wanted proof that Ella was really OK. Then one day a nurse came over to me. She was one of the younger ones. A bright, bonny lass.

"She glanced round to see no-one was looking and then she pushed a photo into my hand. 'Don't tell anyone I gave you this,' she hissed.

"The photo showed Ella all plump and clean. She wasn't smiling. She looked solemn and still. But she seemed to be trying to tell me something. Her eyes were gazing straight into mine.

"I put the photo under my pillow. And that night I slept for the first time in weeks.

"When I woke up I was feeling better. The sun was shining through the hospital window. I was taken to be fitted for a wooden leg.

"After that, my luck took an upward turn. I was due to leave hospital, but where would I go? I thought I should finish up in a home.

"But then something happened. Something good. And I was never to be that unhappy again."

Chapter 7
A New Family

Grandad stopped talking. He was smiling. The smile made him look different. You could nearly imagine him being young.

I tapped his arm. "What happened?" I asked.

"Well, there was this couple who'd read about me. They'd seen my picture in the newspaper. They wanted to find out more about me. They were a couple with no children of their own.

"One day a lady came to see me. She was thin and wore a brown, felt hat. I remember she had this wart on her face. She stared at me where I lay in bed. Then she leaned forward and said loudly, 'There's a very good couple who might like you. You've to be nice to them, d'you understand? You can't go and live with your aunty again. She can't do with you. You're too bad a lad.'

"The lady talked to me as if I was daft. She said everything slowly and too loud. When she spoke her wart wobbled up and down.

"She went on. 'I want you to behave yourself. You're to smile at them. Call them Sir and Madam. If you're good they might want to take you home. Remember that and don't be rude.'

"Well. I was scared and fed-up by what she said. Who was she, anyway? *I* didn't know. And would the new people be like my aunt and uncle? Would they just want someone to do the chores for them?

"I scowled at the lady when she finished speaking. She glared back out of her sharp, brown eyes. Then she leaned even closer and said in my ear, 'They're better than you deserve, young man. Just you remember that when they come.'

"She turned on her heel and stamped out of the ward. Her back looked like an ironing board. You could hear her feet echo in the corridor. There was the sound of a distant door being slammed.

"Two days later she was back again.

'Mr and Mrs Ross are here. Remember what I said to you. Be polite. Don't fidget about. Remember to call them Sir and Madam.'

"She spoke to me like my aunt used to do. Just as if my feelings didn't count. So I folded my arms across my chest. When the couple came in I glared at them. I kept my mouth buttoned up real close.

'You must be Alfred,' the lady said. She had a nut brown face and rosy cheeks. 'Poor Alfred. You've been through the wars, haven't you? Well, never mind. You're all right now. Say hello to my husband. I'm afraid he's shy.'

"Mr Ross shuffled his feet. His neck was too long. He wore glasses. He kept turning his hat round and round in his hands."

'How-do, son,' he said. His face went red. He gave a loud gulp and came forward a step. He held out a shaking hand towards me.

'Well, go on then, Alfred,' Mrs Ross said. 'Shake his hand or he'll be right upset.'

"Slowly I put my own hand out. I let it hover close to Mr Ross's. When his hand took mine it felt warm and dry.

'There now!' Mrs Ross said. 'That didn't hurt much, did it, lads?'

"She pulled a chair up and sat down on it. After that *she* took a hold of my hand. She spoke to me in a very soft and kind voice.

'I know we're not Ella. She's special to you. But we can still be your friends, Alfred. Is that all right?'

"My head seemed to nod of its own accord. I reckon I was even forgetting to glare. Mrs Ross squeezed my hand very tightly in hers. I heard Mr Ross give a great loud cough.

"In the end, I went home with them. Only not right then, it took a week or two to sort it all out.

"I had to get used to my new leg first. After that I had to practise walking."

"And did you ever see Ella again?" I asked.

Grandad shook his head. "Only in my mind. I'll just hear a laugh or feel this warmth. She's never really gone away. She's inside my head like a patch of sun."

"Yeah." I looked at the floor. I didn't know whether to feel happy or sad. "Can I see Ella's photo now?" I asked.

Grandad fumbled in a bedside drawer and took out a scruffy, leather wallet. Inside the wallet was the photograph.

It was just a baby like any other. Maybe the eyes looked a little bit wider. Maybe there was something about the chin.

"She looks like our mum!" I said, surprised.

"Your mum was the image of her when she was born. I couldn't get over it. It was like magic again. We called her Joy, because that's what she was. It seemed right then and it seems right now."

Grandad traced the photo with the tip of his finger. He seemed to have forgotten I was there.

Very slowly I got to my feet. I thought Grandad wanted to be left alone. But when I got to the door he looked up and spoke.

"Take care of your brother! D'you hear me, Mick?"

I nodded silently and went back downstairs.

Chapter 8
The End

A few days later Pete came round. "Is Joe in?" he asked me.

I shrugged. "Dunno."

"We were going to go off round the park – can he borrow your bike? His own's too small."

I opened my mouth, then closed it again. I remembered what Grandad had said. *Take care of your brother.* It made me think.

Joe's OK, really. Most of the time. We mess about. We tease our mum. When the chips are down he's on my side.

If Joe went away I'd be really upset. I'd miss him like an arm or a leg. He's kind of special, like no-one else. It's not his fault he's so popular.

"Well?" said Pete. "Can Joe borrow your bike, just for this morning, like?"

I glared at him and folded my arms. "No!" I yelled. "He flaming well can't! He'll have to use his own stupid bike!"

Who is Barrington Stoke?

Barrington Stoke was a famous and much-loved story-teller. He travelled from village to village carrying a lantern to light his way. He arrived as it grew dark and when the young boys and girls of the village saw the glow of his lantern, they hurried to the central meeting place. They were full of excitement and expectation, for his stories were always wonderful.

Then Barrington Stoke set down his lantern. In the flickering light the listeners were enthralled by his tales of adventure, horror and mystery. He knew exactly what they liked best and he loved telling a good story. And another. And then another. When the lantern burned low and dawn was nearly breaking, he slipped away. He was gone by morning, only to appear the next day in some other village to tell the next story.

Barrington Stoke would like to thank all its readers for commenting on the manuscript before publication and in particular:

Danyelle Abbott
Ardit Alia
James Bellamy
Chloe Berndt
Larissa Brett
George Castle
Joanna Childs
Harry Cliff
William Collins
Christine Cook
Billy Daniels
Ben Davies
Simon East
George Eva
Tom Flanagan
John Flothmann
Christopher Keenan
Oliver Kempton
Andrew Knowles

Gail Macleod
Steven Mallett
Domenic Marra
Matthew Marshall
Jonathan McNamee
Corinne Mitchell
James Morris
Jenny Murphy
Brendan Pollitt
Laura Purcell
Joseph Senior
Michael Sinclair
Declan Sutch
Edward Louis Villiers
Vaughan Walton
Ryan Watson
Ashley Webber
Josie Williamson
Sarah Louise Wood
J Young

Become a Consultant!

Would you like to give us feedback on our titles before they are published? Contact us at the address or website below – we'd love to hear from you!

Barrington Stoke, 10 Belford Terrace, Edinburgh EH4 3DQ
Tel: 0131 315 4933 Fax: 0131 315 4934
E-mail: info@barringtonstoke.co.uk
Website: www.barringtonstoke.co.uk

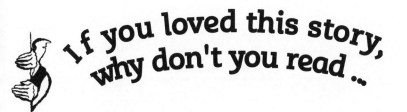

If you loved this story, why don't you read ..

Bungee Hero
by Julie Bertagna

Are you afraid of heights? Adam is terrified of them. So why then would he do a bungee jump to earn money for charity? It is only after old Mr Haddock tells him his sad story that Adam decides to take the plunge. But will he just be too scared to do it?

You can order this book directly from
Macmillan Distribution Ltd, Brunel Road, Houndmills,
Basingstoke, Hampshire RG21 6XS
Tel: 01256 302699

If you loved this story, why don't you read ..

Resistance
by Ann Jungman

Do you ever disagree with your parents? Jan is ashamed when his Dutch father sides with the Germans during the Second World War. No-one will talk to him at school. Only Elli is his friend. Can Jan find a way to defy his father and help the Resistance?

You can order this book directly from
Macmillan Distribution Ltd, Brunel Road, Houndmills,
Basingstoke, Hampshire RG21 6XS
Tel: 01256 302699